Doctor

Quarto is the authority on a wide range of topics.

Quarto educates, entertains and enriches the lives of our readers—enthusiasts and lovers of hands-on living.

www.quartoknows.com

Leabharlann

Contae na Midhe

First published in the UK in 2009 by
QED Publishing
Part of The Quarto Group
The Old Brewery
6 Blundell Street
London, N7 9BH

A catalogue record for this book is available from the British Library.

ISBN 978 1 84835 250 6

Printed and bound in China

Author Amanda Askew
Designer and Illustrator Andrew Crowson
Consultants Shirley Bickler and Tracey Dils

Publisher Steve Evans
Creative Director Zeta Davies
Managing Editor Amanda Askew

Words in bold are explained in the glossary on page 24.

People who help us

Doctor

Amanda Askew
Andrew Crowson

QED

Meet Amar. He is a doctor. He helps to make sick people feel better.

When Dr Amar arrives at the **surgery**, Tanya is there. Tanya looks after the office and makes sure that everything is ready for when the **patients** arrive.

"Here's your mail."
"Thanks, Tanya."

Dr Amar goes into his office. He has a desk, chairs, cupboards and a consulting bed.

He looks at his computer to check which patients he will see today.

Dr Amar's first patient is Rosie. She has a sore throat and a **fever**.

"Your throat is very red with yellow spots. You'll have to have a few days off school and take some **medicine**."

Dr Amar prints out a **prescription** from the computer and hands it to Rosie's dad.

"Please get this medicine from the **chemist**."

Next, Edward comes in. He has been getting headaches when he watches television or reads the newspaper.

Dr Amar gives him an eye test.

"A, T... the others are a little blurry."

"I'd like you to visit an **optician** to see if you need glasses. Then come back to see me if you're still getting headaches."

11

Dr Amar sees about 15 people in the morning, but not everyone is ill.

Last week, Jane fell off her bike and cut her arm deeply. She has come back to see Dr Amar today to check that her arm is **healing** properly.

"It's looking good. I'll put a clean **bandage** on and see you again next week."

Next, Rory and his younger brother come in for a check-up.

Rory is five years old. "Hello Rory. Step on the scales for me. You weigh 18 kilograms. You're growing quickly!"

Rory's brother is three years old. Dr Amar gives him a special **injection** to stop him from getting serious illnesses.

"James, sit on Mummy's knee and read this book while I give you an injection."

"All finished. Well done for being a brave boy."

In the afternoon, Dr Amar
sees about 15 more people.

Salma has itchy **eczema** on her arms
that she cannot stop scratching.

Peter has terrible earache.

Brad has a rash.

Susi has a
tickly cough.

21

Finally, Dr Amar sees Tom. He has banged his thumb with a hammer. It's very red and swollen.

Dr Amar cleans his thumb and wraps it in a bandage.

"Come back to see me if the swelling does not go down in a few days."

Glossary

Bandage A piece of cloth that is tied around a cut to protect it.

Chemist A shop that sells medicine.

Eczema Where the skin is very red, swollen and itchy.

Fever A high temperature.

Heal When skin or bone grows back and becomes healthy again.

Injection Where a needle is used to put medicine into someone's body.

Medicine A liquid that someone drinks to get well.

Optician Someone who checks that people can see properly.

Patient Someone who visits a doctor when they are sick.

Prescription A piece of paper that tells a chemist which medicine someone needs.

Surgery A place where a doctor sees patients.